I Love You, Bunny Rabbit

I Love You, Bunny Rabbit

by Shulamith Levey Oppenheim
pictures by Cyd Moore

A Picture Yearling Book

For Micah and Noah with love

—S.L.O.

For my parents

—C.M.

Published by
Bantam Doubleday Dell Books for Young Readers
a division of
Bantam Doubleday Dell Publishing Group, Inc.
1540 Broadway
New York, New York 10036

ISBN: 0-440-41172-6
Reprinted by arrangement with Boyds Mills Press
Printed in the United States of America

March 1997
10 9 8 7 6 5 4 3

This is Micah's rabbit.
Her name is Bunny Rabbit.

She has no fur.
She is made of stuffed flannel.
She has eaten applesauce.
She has drunk chocolate milk.
She has swum in mud puddles.
She has been thoroughly chewed.

"It is time," Micah's mama says,
"to wash this rabbit."

"Don't worry." Micah kisses Bunny Rabbit.
"I've had lots of baths. They're not so bad."

Micah climbs up on his stool.
Mama fills the washbasin with warm water.
Micah pours in some sweet-smelling soap.
The water is very sudsy.
"Here we go." Very gently he puts Bunny Rabbit into the water.

"Does her head go under the water?" Micah asks. "I don't think she can hold her breath."
Mama smiles. "No, we'll wipe it off with a washcloth the way we do yours. But we won't touch her ears until I mend them. They look as if they'd just dissolve in the water."

"How long will she have to soak?"
"A few minutes," Mama answers.
She takes a nail brush and scrubs the stains.
"Let's take her out now, please. She's cold!"

Micah squeezes Bunny Rabbit.
The applesauce is still there.
The chocolate milk is still there.
The puddle mud is still there.

"We'll wait until she's dry," Mama says.

The next morning Mama says,

"Bunny Rabbit is a mess. The stains are there. Her ears won't mend. The flannel is worn to the stuffing. It is time, Micah, to buy a new rabbit."

Mama buttons up Micah's sweater.
She pulls on his high red boots.
Yesterday it rained.

"Don't worry." Micah tucks Bunny Rabbit into the pocket of his sweater. "Don't worry, because *I* love you, Bunny Rabbit."

On the way to the toy store
Micah jumps over a puddle.
"Mama, sometimes boys
and girls fall right into the
middle of a mud puddle."

Micah stares up at Mama.
He takes her hand.
They go to the toy store.

TOYS

"Over there." The salesperson
points to the wall. "You'll find
a zoo of stuffed animals."
Micah pats Bunny Rabbit.
"Don't worry," he whispers.

Micah's mama takes his hand.
They stand and look.
There are many, many rabbits.
Big ones and little ones.
Flop-eared ones and lop-eared ones.
White ones with pink eyes.

Brown ones with black eyes.
Some have clothes on and some don't.
Some are wearing glasses and some are not.
Some are lying down and some are sitting up
and some are standing.

“Take your time.”
Mama unbuttons Micah’s sweater.
“I don’t want a new rabbit, thank you.”
He looks up at Mama. She looks down at him.
“Bunny Rabbit is a mess, Micah.”
“I know,” answers Micah.
He pulls Bunny Rabbit from his pocket.
He presses her against his chest.
“I love you, Bunny Rabbit,” he says very quietly.

Mama is standing very still.
She buttons up Micah's sweater.
"Would you like a milk shake?"
Her voice is soft and quiet.

She smooths the hair away from Micah's eyes.
"Yes, please." Micah tucks Bunny Rabbit
back into his pocket.

On the way home Micah says,
"Sometimes I get very sticky
drinking milk shakes."

He shakes his finger in the air.
"And sometimes you say
'Ugh, you look so messy, Micah!'"

Mama stops.
She takes Micah in her arms.
"I love you, Micah Gregory," Mama whispers.
"I love you, too . . . and Bunny Rabbit," Micah shouts.